LIFE IN THE AMAZON JUNGLE

Alan Trussell-Cullen

Australia • Brazil • Japan • Korea • Mexico • Singapore • Spain • United Kingdom • United States

Life in the Amazon Jungle

Fast Forward
Gold Level 21

Text: Alan Trussell-Cullen
Editor: Bec Quinn
Design: James Lowe
Series design: James Lowe
Production controller: Seona Galbally
Photo research: Michelle Cottrill
Audio recordings: Juliet Hill, Picture Start
Spoken by: Matthew King and Abbe Holmes
Reprint: Siew Han Ong

Acknowledgements
The author and publisher would like to acknowledge permission to reproduce material from the following sources: Photographs by Auscape/ John Cancalosi, p 14 left/ Francois Gohier, p 10 left/ Jacques Jangoux, p 23/ Schafer & Hill – Peter Arnold, p 11 right/ Theo Allofs, pp 16 right, 18 top/ Tui De Roy, p 11 left; Photolibrary/ Animals Animals/ Doug Wechsler, pp 12–13 (background)/ Animals Animals/ Marion Bacon, p. 13 left/ Animals Animals/ David Lazenby, p 17 left/ Animals Animals/ Nigel J H Smith, pp 10–11 (background)/ Carey Alan, front cover bottom, pp 1 bottom, 15 right/ David Aubrey, p 15 left/ Dr Morley Read, pp 4 right, 14 right/ Eric Horan, p 12 left/ George Bernard, pp 16–17 (background)/ Gregory MD, pp 3, 13 right/ IFA-Bilderteam GMBH, p 16 left/ Inga Spence, p 5 right/ Jacques Jangoux, pp 4–5 (background), 22, 6–7 (background), 9 right/ Joe Macdonald, p 18 bottom/ Luiz C. Marigo, p 5 left/ Mark Jones, pp 8–9 (background)/ Michael Fogden, pp 10 right, 14–15 (background)/ Natures Images, p 17 right/ Nick Gordon, p 19/ TC Nature, p 4 left/ Tom Brakefield, p 12 right/ Victor Englebert, front and back cover, pp 1 top, 20–21.

ISBN 978 0 17 012677 9
ISBN 978 0 17 012669 4 (set)

Cengage Learning Australia
Level 7, 80 Dorcas Street
South Melbourne, Victoria Australia 3205
Phone: 1300 790 853

Cengage Learning New Zealand
Unit 4B Rosedale Office Park
331 Rosedale Road, Albany, North Shore NZ 0632
Phone: 0508 635 766

For learning solutions, visit cengage.com.au

Printed in Australia by Ligare Pty Ltd
7 8 9 10 11 12 13 21 20 19 18 17

Evaluated in independent research by staff from the Department of Language, Literacy and Arts Education at the University of Melbourne.

LIFE IN THE AMAZON JUNGLE

Alan Trussell-Cullen

Contents

Chapter 1

AN AMAZING TREASURE TROVE

The Amazon Jungle teems with life.
It is home to more different **species**
of plants and animals
than any other place on Earth –
over 4000 kinds of trees,
three million kinds of insects, 500 species of **mammals**,
and at least one-third of the world's birds.

a herrania tree

a hyacinth macaw

an emperor tamarin

a pink ginger flower

Every year scientists discover hundreds of new plants and animals in the Amazon Jungle.
No wonder scientists call the Amazon Jungle an amazing **treasure trove**.

Chapter 2

TROPICAL RAINFORESTS

The Amazon Jungle is a tropical rainforest. Tropical rainforests can be found in many parts of the world, but they are all very similar.

It is warm and wet in tropical rainforests. The temperature stays between 20°C and 30°C all year round.

It rains a lot in tropical rainforests, too. Tropical rainforests get at least one-and-a-half metres of rain each year.

Tropical rainforests all have a huge number of different plants and animals living close together. In one acre of forest there might be over 300 species of trees, and hundreds of species of animals, birds and insects.

Chapter 3

THE AMAZON JUNGLE: FROM THE TREETOPS TO THE GROUND

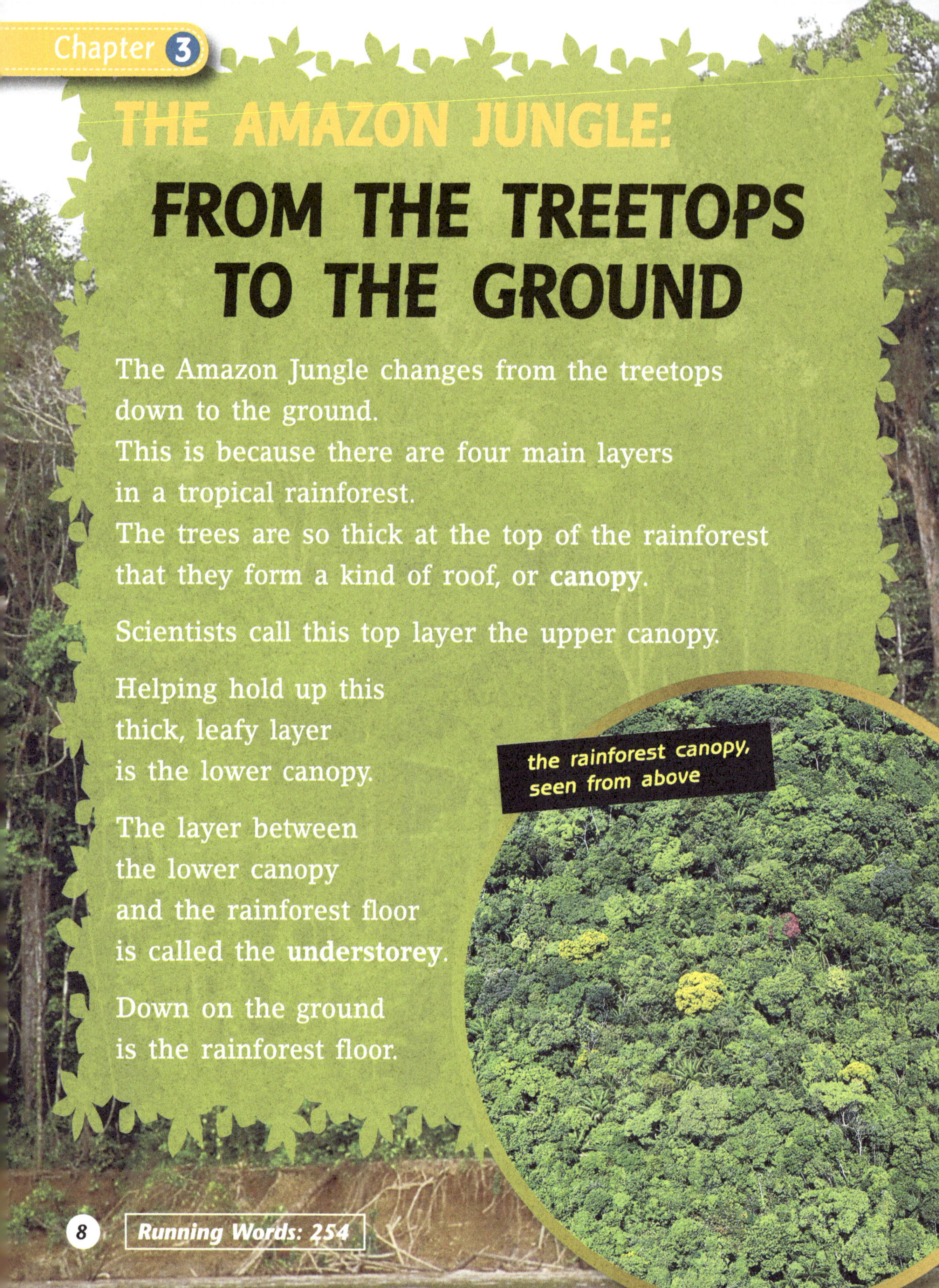

The Amazon Jungle changes from the treetops down to the ground.
This is because there are four main layers in a tropical rainforest.
The trees are so thick at the top of the rainforest that they form a kind of roof, or **canopy**.

Scientists call this top layer the upper canopy.

Helping hold up this thick, leafy layer is the lower canopy.

The layer between the lower canopy and the rainforest floor is called the **understorey**.

Down on the ground is the rainforest floor.

the rainforest canopy, seen from above

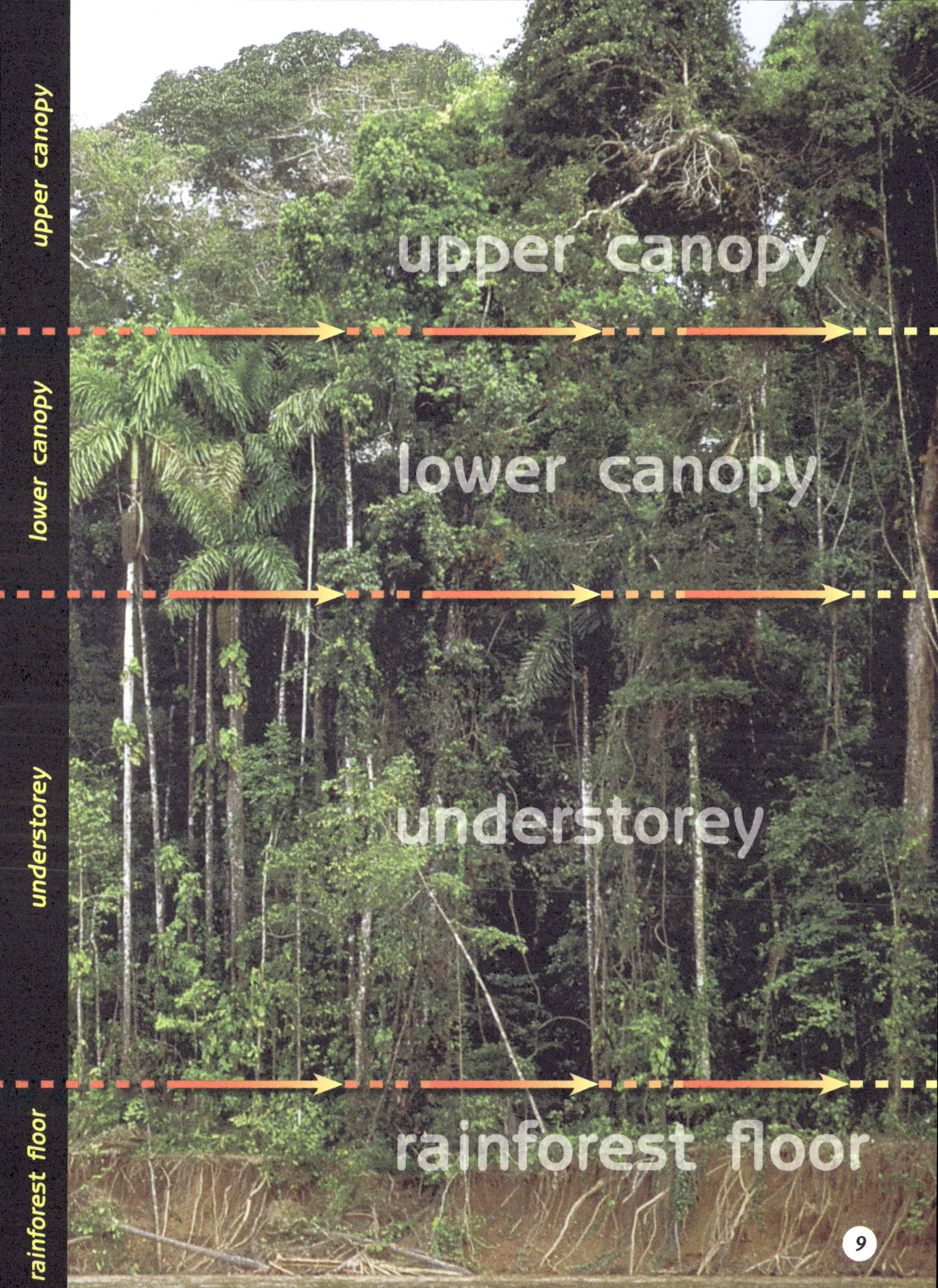
upper canopy
lower canopy
understorey
rainforest floor
upper canopy
lower canopy
understorey
rainforest floor

Life in the Upper Canopy

At the top of the rainforest, the trees crowd together as they struggle to catch the sunlight.

Many different kinds of flowers and fruits grow here, so there is lots of food for all kinds of insects, animals and birds.

a morpho butterfly

a scarlet macaw

Macaws fly by in a flash of red, blue and yellow. There are toucans with their huge colourful beaks. Harpy eagles circle above as they hunt for smaller birds, monkeys, sloths and other animals of the forest.

Life in the Lower Canopy

The strong branches that hold up the canopy
can be seen under the leafy top layer of the rainforest.
Large animals use these branches
to move around the rainforest.
Here, in the early mornings or late afternoons,
squirrel monkeys swing from tree to tree
in noisy groups, as they look for fruit to eat.

a squirrel monkey

a howler monkey

Sloths also hang from these branches. They stay so still that it is hard see them move at all.

There are also snakes like the emerald tree boa, which slither along the huge branches looking for food.

an emerald tree boa

a two-toed sloth

Life in the Understorey

It is darker in the understorey than in the upper or lower canopy. Smaller trees, shrubs, palms and ferns grow against the tall trunks of the bigger trees.

an imababura tree frog

a tropical caterpillar

Fewer animals make their homes in this part of the rainforest, because it is so dark. But many animals, such as monkeys, sloths and fruit bats, swing, climb or fly through it.

Small birds are safe from large **predators** here, and many make their nests in the understorey.

a scarlet violet-ear hummingbird

an anteater

Life on the Rainforest Floor

It is very dark down on the rainforest floor. Only about five per cent of the sunlight gets through the thick layers of leaves and branches above, so only a few small plants can grow here. But hundreds of species of fungi grow well in this dark part of the jungle.

orange fungi on the rainforest floor

leafcutter ants

The rainforest floor is covered with leaves, fallen branches and fruit.
Spiders and insects make their homes here.
Birds go scratching in the fallen leaves.
Lizards and frogs wait for insects to come by.

a tarantula spider

an Amazon horned toad

Some large predators use the rainforest floor to hide so they can catch their **prey**. Boa constrictors hide until they see their prey, then they wrap themselves around their prey and squeeze it before eating it whole.

A boa constrictor squeezing its prey.

Jaguars are silent night hunters,
but they also catch fish in streams during the day.
They wait by the water
and quickly snatch fish when they swim by.

a jaguar

Chapter 4

PEOPLE AND THE AMAZON JUNGLE

For hundreds of years, the **indigenous people** living in the Amazon Jungle have used many of its plants for food and medicine. Today, scientists are discovering how amazing some of these plants are.

Hundreds of new medicines are now being tested and made from plants found in the Amazon. They are being used to treat people with cancer, diabetes, AIDS and other diseases.

However, people cause problems for the rainforest. People are clearing the Amazon Jungle for farmland. Twenty per cent of the jungle has already been lost in this way.

Many of the world's rainforests are being cleared.
Once, rainforests covered 14 per cent of the Earth's surface, but now they cover only six per cent.
Every day, people cut down, burn or clear 13 000 acres of rainforest, and scientists say that every day, over 130 plant, animal and insect species are lost from the planet forever.

Fire is used to clear the rainforest.

This is what people can do to help save the world's remaining rainforests:

- Find out what is happening in the world's rainforests.
- Tell others what is happening in the world's rainforests.
- Try not to use **products** that destroy the rainforest.

logging in the Amazon rainforest

Glossary

canopy	a roof-like cover hanging over something
indigenous people	the first people to live in a place
mammals	animals whose young feed on milk from their mother's breast
predators	animals that eat other animals
prey	an animal killed by another animal for food
products	things people make
species	a group of plants or animals that are the same
treasure trove	a collection of valuable things
understorey	the area of a forest that grows in the shade of the canopy

Index